Dear Parent:

Congratulations! Your child is taking the first steps on an exciting journey. The destination? Independent reading!

STEP INTO READING® will help your child get there. The program offers five steps to reading success. Each step includes fun stories and colorful art. There are also Step into Reading Sticker Books, Step into Reading Math Readers, Step into Reading Write-In Readers, Step into Reading Phonics Readers, and Step into Reading Phonics First Steps! Boxed Sets—a complete literacy program with something for every child.

Learning to Read, Step by Step!

Ready to Read Preschool–Kindergarten
• big type and easy words • rhyme and rhythm • picture clues
For children who know the alphabet and are eager to begin reading.

Reading with Help Preschool–Grade 1
• basic vocabulary • short sentences • simple stories
For children who recognize familiar words and sound out new words with help.

Reading on Your Own Grades 1–3
• engaging characters • easy-to-follow plots • popular topics
For children who are ready to read on their own.

Reading Paragraphs Grades 2–3
• challenging vocabulary • short paragraphs • exciting stories
For newly independent readers who read simple sentences with confidence.

Ready for Chapters Grades 2–4
• chapters • longer paragraphs • full-color art
For children who want to take the plunge into chapter books but still like colorful pictures.

STEP INTO READING® is designed to give every child a successful reading experience. The grade levels are only guides. Children can progress through the steps at their own speed, developing confidence in their reading, no matter what their grade.

Remember, a lifetime love of reading starts with a single step!

For Mom, my very best friend
—M.L.

www.stepintoreading.com
Educators and librarians, for a variety of teaching tools, visit us at
www.randomhouse.com/teachers

Library of Congress Cataloging-in-Publication Data
Lagonegro, Melissa.
   Friends for a princess / by Melissa Lagonegro ; illustrated by Atelier Philippe Harchy.
      p. cm. — (Step into reading. A step 1 book)
SUMMARY: Easy-to-read rhyming text describes Snow White's seven little friends.
ISBN 0-7364-2208-0 — ISBN 0-7364-8027-7 (Gibraltar Library Edition : alk. paper)
[1. Dwarfs—Fiction. 2. Princesses—Fiction. 3. Friendship—Fiction. 4. Stories in rhyme.]
I. Atelier Philippe Harchy, ill. II. Title. III. Series: Step into reading. Step 1 book
   PZ8.3.L214Fr 2004
[E]—dc21   2003004916

Printed in the United States of America 10

STEP INTO READING, RANDOM HOUSE, and the Random House colophon are registered trademarks of Random House, Inc.

DISNEP
✦ PRINCESS

Friends for a Princess

By Melissa Lagonegro
Illustrated by Atelier Philippe Harchy

Random House 🏠 New York

Snow White has
seven little friends.
Loving, kind,
and special friends.

Some have big beards.

Some have small.

Dopey has no beard at all.

Doc is caring.

Doc is wise.

Doc needs glasses for his eyes.

Happy is
the cheerful guy.

Bashful is
so very shy.

Sneezy always
has to sneeze.

Grumpy is
so hard to please.

Sleepy likes to
take a nap.

Dopey wears a
purple cap.

All the Dwarfs
work in a mine.

Then they march
home in a line.

Snow White is there
when they come back.

She welcomes them
and makes a snack.

The jolly friends
dance through the night.

The Seven Dwarfs
love sweet Snow White.

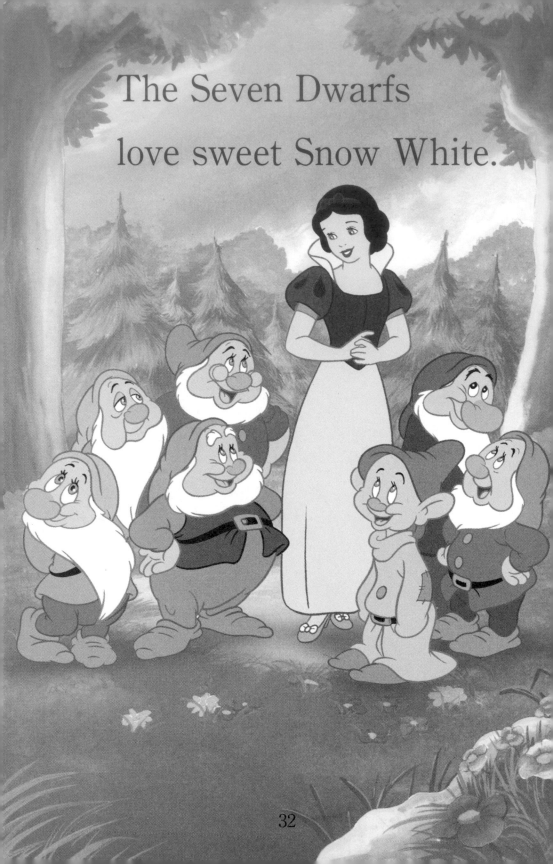